Published in the United States by Random House Children's Books,
a division of Random House, Inc., 1745 Broadway, New York, NY 10019,
and in Canada by Random House of Canada Limited, Toronto,
in conjunction with Disney Enterprises, Inc. Random House and the
colophon are registered trademarks and A Stepping Stone Book
and the colophon are trademarks of Random House, Inc.

Library of Congress Cataloging-in-Publication Data

Richards, Kitty.
Woody's wild adventure / by Kitty Richards.
p. cm.
"A Stepping Stone Book."
ISBN 978-0-7364-2666-4 (trade) — ISBN 978-0-7364-8077-2 (lib. bdg.)
I. Toy story 3 (Motion picture). II. Title.
PZ7.R387 Wo 2010
[Fic]—dc22
2009038677

www.randomhouse.com/kids

Printed in the United States of America

10   9   8   7   6   5   4   3   2   1

Disney · PIXAR

TOY STORY 3

WOODY'S
WILD ADVENTURE

A STEPPING STONE BOOK™

Random House 🏠 New York

DISNEP · PIXAR

TOY STORY 3

WOODY'S WILD ADVENTURE

Adapted by Kitty Richards
Illustrated by Dan Gracey

We huddled in the dark toy box. I checked to make sure everyone was in place— Buzz Lightyear, Jessie, Mr. and Mrs. Potato Head, Slinky Dog, Hamm, Rex, Bullseye, and the Aliens. We couldn't make any mistakes. We would only have one shot at this.

Sarge and his men came into Andy's room, dragging a gym sock. They lifted it up to the toy box, and Andy's cell phone slid out.

"Mission accomplished!" Sarge said.

Rex held the cell phone as Buzz pulled out a cordless phone that we had swiped from Andy's kitchen earlier that day. Jessie punched in the numbers.

The cell phone began to ring. We all stared at the door, waiting. "Just like we rehearsed it, guys," I said as I closed the toy box lid.

We heard footsteps running up the stairs. Then the door to Andy's room creaked open. We could hear Andy shuffling around as he looked for his cell phone.

Suddenly the lid of the toy box opened and Andy's face appeared, looking down at us. Andy was a teenager, but he still had the same kind face he'd had ever since he was a little boy.

He reached for his phone. It was still clutched between Rex's tiny dinosaur arms. Andy picked up Rex and yanked the phone free. He put it to his ear.

"Hello?" he said. He waited. "Anyone there?"

No answer, of course. Andy snapped his phone closed. He stared down at Rex for a moment.

I held my breath. Would our plan work? Andy hadn't played with us in years. But maybe now he would. Maybe we'd get one last playtime. . . .

No such luck. Andy tossed Rex back into the toy box. He shut the lid and left the room.

Disappointed, we pushed open the lid and piled out of the box.

"Well, *that* went well," Mr. Potato Head said sarcastically.

"He held me! He actually held me!" Rex cried.

Hamm rolled his eyes. "Oh, this is just sad."

"We all knew Operation Playtime was a long shot," I reminded them.

"But we can try again, right?" asked Rex.

I sighed. It was time to tell everyone the truth. "I'm calling it, guys," I said. "We're closing up shop. Andy's going to college any day now. That was our last shot."

The toys all groaned.

"We're going into Attic Mode, folks," Buzz said. "Keep your accessories with you at all times. Spare parts, batteries—anything you need for an orderly transition."

Mr. Potato Head frowned at him. "Orderly?

Don't you get it? We're done! Finished! Over the hill!"

I tried to calm everyone down. "Hey, hey, hey. Now come on, guys, we all knew this day was coming."

"Yeah, but now it's here!" moaned Hamm, the coins in his piggy-bank belly jingling.

"Look, every toy goes through this," I explained. "No one wants to see their kid grow up and leave!"

Suddenly Buzz called out, "Hey, Sarge! What are you doing?"

We all spun around. Sarge and his last two soldiers were climbing to the windowsill.

"We've done our duty," said Sarge. "Andy's grown up."

"And let's face it," a soldier added. "When the trash bags come out, we army guys are the first to go."

"Who said anything about trash bags?" I exclaimed.

"It has been an honor serving with you,"

Sarge replied humbly. "Good luck, folks."

"Yeah, you're gonna need it," said the soldier. They jumped out the window, their parachutes opening. We watched in shock.

"No, no, no, no, no!" I yelled. "Come back!"

"We're getting thrown away?" Rex asked. He looked positively terrified.

Jessie was so upset she could hardly breathe. "We're being abandoned!"

Everyone started talking and yelling at once. "Quiet!" I shouted. They stopped and listened.

"Look, we're all still here, aren't we?" I said. "I mean, yeah, we've lost friends along the way." They knew I was talking about Wheezy and Etch. And my sweet Bo Peep. "But through every yard sale, every spring cleaning, Andy has held on to *us*. He must care about us, or we wouldn't be here."

A few toys nodded.

"You wait," I told them. "Andy is going to tuck us into the attic. It'll be safe and warm."

"And we'll all be together," added Buzz.

"Don't worry," I insisted. "Andy's going to take care of us. I guarantee it."

The toys didn't look happy, but I knew I'd convinced them. Reluctantly, they headed off to collect their spare parts.

I took a look around the room. So many things had changed over the years. Now posters of rock groups hung on the walls. A guitar and skateboard sat where toys used to be.

On Andy's bulletin board, I caught a glimpse of an old photo: ten-year-old Andy playing with Buzz and me and the rest of the toys. That was the best time of our lives.

I meant what I'd told the other toys. I knew Andy would take care of us. But still, I couldn't help wishing that things could go back to the way they used to be.

The next thing we knew, Andy was coming back up the stairs. We scrambled into the toy box just in time.

Andy sat down at his desk and began typing on his laptop. Just then, his mom walked into the room carrying cardboard boxes and a package of trash bags.

"Okay, Andy, let's get to work here," she said. "Anything you're not taking to college either goes in the attic, or it's trash." We watched as she wrote COLLEGE on one of the boxes in black marker.

Andy didn't even glance up from the computer screen. "Mom, I'm not leaving until Friday," he complained.

"Come on," she said. "It's garbage day." She

lifted the toy box lid. "What are you going to do with these toys?" she asked. "Should we donate them to Sunnyside?"

"No," said Andy.

"Maybe sell them online?" suggested his mom.

Andy shook his head. "Mom, no one's going to want those old toys. They're junk."

A shock went right through me. *Junk! Did he say junk?* I knew Andy couldn't have meant that!

"Fine," said his mom. "You have until Friday. Anything that's not packed for college, or in the attic, is getting thrown out."

"Whatever you say, Mom," Andy replied.

The next thing we knew, Andy was staring down into the toy box at us. Suddenly, he grabbed a trash bag and . . . one by one he started dumping toys inside!

Finally, the only toys left were Buzz and I. Andy held us, one in each hand, considering. Then he tossed me into the college box . . . and dropped Buzz into the garbage bag.

I popped my head out of the box and saw Andy carrying the bag out of the room. Was he really throwing the toys away? I scrambled after him. In the hallway, he stopped. He pulled open the retractable ladder that led to the attic. I breathed a sigh of relief. Andy wasn't throwing the bag away. My friends were going into storage! Everything was going to be okay. . . .

Just then, Andy's little sister, Molly, walked by. She was struggling to carry a heavy box of toys that she was donating to the local daycare center. Andy left his bag of toys at the bottom of the ladder and helped her carry the box down the stairs.

Suddenly, the spring-loaded ladder began to close. It knocked over the bag of toys. Before I could do anything to help, Andy's mom came into the hallway and tripped over the bag.

"Andy!" she said, annoyed. She picked the bag up and took it downstairs with the rest of the trash she was carrying. This was not good.

"That's not trash!" I cried. I could hear the rumble of the garbage truck coming up the street. I had to act quickly!

I ran into Andy's room and climbed to the windowsill. The truck was getting closer! I grabbed a pair of scissors from Andy's desk and shoved them into my holster. Then I jumped out the window, sliding down the drainpipe outside.

By the time I got to the curb, the garbage truck was pulling up to the house. I ran to one of the bags and stabbed it with the scissors.

Trash spilled out. Wrong bag. I tried another. No luck. More trash.

Suddenly, the garbageman grabbed all the bags, dumped them into the truck, and took off.

The truck stopped at the next house. The garbageman yanked a lever and the truck's compactor lowered . . . and crushed the trash bags!

"Buzz!" I cried in horror. "Jessie!" I was devastated. My friends were gone.

Just then I heard a noise. I spun around and saw the recycling bin moving toward the garage on little toy feet. *Whew!*

I quickly crossed the yard. But when I got to the garage, I saw something strange. My friends were climbing into the donation box in Andy's mom's car!

"Buzz? What's going on?" I said. "Don't you know this box is being donated?"

"It's under control, Woody," said Buzz. "We have a plan!"

"We're going to daycare!" Rex added.

I was shocked. "Daycare? Have you lost all your marbles?"

"Didn't you see?" replied Mrs. Potato Head. "Andy threw us away!"

"No!" I shouted. "That was a mistake! Andy was taking you to the attic."

"Yeah. After he called us junk," Hamm grumbled.

"Oh, come on!" I protested. "He didn't mean that."

"He put us in a garbage bag and left us on the curb," Jessie said angrily.

"Yeah, I know it looks bad. But, guys, you have to believe me!" I pleaded.

Mr. Potato Head rolled his eyes. "Sure thing, college boy."

"Andy's moving on, Woody," said Jessie. "It's time we did the same." And with that, the rest of the toys climbed into the box.

That's when I lost my patience. Enough was enough! "Okay, out of the box!" I hollered. "Everyone, right now! Come on! Buzz, give me

a hand. We have to get this thing out of here!" I tried to push the box out of the car.

Jessie glared at me, and I glared right back. Buzz stepped between us. "Woody, wait!" he said. "We need to figure out what's best for everyone—"

SLAM! Suddenly, Andy's mom closed the car's hatchback and got inside. We heard the engine start. A second later, the car pulled out of the driveway and onto the street.

"Oh, great!" I wailed. "It's going to take us forever to get back here!"

Buzz and I climbed into the box. I tried to reason with the toys, but no one was listening. They were gathered around Barbie, one of Molly's toys. Barbie was as upset as my friends.

I told them all that daycare was a sad and lonely place for washed-up toys who had no owners. But no one wanted to believe me.

We'd find out who was right soon enough.

The car pulled into the parking lot of the daycare center. Andy's mom picked us up and started toward the building.

Inside the crowded box, everyone was trying to get a look through the handles. I caught a quick glimpse of a redbrick building. The sign in front read SUNNYSIDE. We could hear children shouting and laughing on the other side of the playground wall.

"See, Woody," said Rex eagerly. "It's nice! The door has a rainbow on it!"

Jessie grinned from ear to ear. "We hit the jackpot, Bullseye!"

I wasn't so sure.

At the front desk, Andy's mom dropped us off with the receptionist. The receptionist's daughter, Bonnie, was there, too. I could see the little girl sitting on top of the desk, playing with a toy monkey.

We didn't stay there for long. The receptionist carried us into a classroom and set the box on a ledge. The room was empty. All the kids were outside playing.

"So, now what do we do?" asked Hamm.

"We go back to Andy's," I told him. "Anyone see an exit?"

"Exit, schmexit!" said Mr. Potato Head. "Let's get played with!"

Everyone started pushing forward to get a look. Suddenly, the whole box tilted and fell off the ledge. We crashed to the floor.

When I looked up, I saw that each and every toy in the room had turned around to stare at us. I gulped. What if they weren't friendly?

"New toys!" one of them shouted. They all cheered and greeted us with open arms.

Honk! Honk! Suddenly a truck raced across the room. It screeched to a stop and spun around.

A big pink teddy bear was sitting in the back.

"Well, hello there," the bear said cheerfully. "I thought I heard new voices! Welcome to Sunnyside, folks. I'm Lots-o'-Huggin' Bear. But please, call me Lotso!"

Buzz stepped forward and held out his hand. "Buzz Lightyear," he said. "We come in pea—"

Lotso scooped Buzz up in a giant bear hug. He lifted the space ranger right off the ground.

"First thing you have to know about me is— I'm a hugger!" the bear said with a chuckle.

Lotso set Buzz back down and smiled at the rest of us. "Oh, look at y'all! You've been through a lot today, haven't you?" he said sympathetically.

"It's been horrible!" said Mrs. Potato Head.

"Well, you're safe now," said Lotso. "We're all cast-offs here. But just you wait. You'll find being donated was the best thing that ever happened to you!"

"What happens when the kids grow up?" Jessie wanted to know.

Lotso led us over to a wall. It was covered in classroom photos of daycare kids.

"When the kids get old, new ones come in," Lotso explained. "You'll never be outgrown or neglected. Never abandoned or forgotten. No owners means no heartbreak."

Jessie's whole face lit up. "Yee-haw!"

"And you wanted to stay at Andy's!" Mr. Potato Head scolded me.

"Because we're *Andy's* toys!" I exclaimed.

The big pink bear put his arm around me. "So you got donated by this 'Andy,' huh? Well, it's his loss, Sheriff! He can't hurt you anymore."

What? This guy had it all wrong! But Lotso didn't give me a chance to explain. He turned to the others. "Now, let's get you all settled in."

He called to a Ken doll, who appeared in the window of a big dollhouse.

"Be there in a jiff!" Ken yelled back. He rode the elevator down, came out of the house, and greeted us. "Who's ready for the tour?" he asked.

But Ken didn't get far before he spotted Barbie. Let's just say, sparks flew. It was love at first sight.

Lotso finally had to break up the love scene. "Let's show our new friends where they'll be staying!" he told Ken.

My friends followed Ken and Lotso, so I went along. Even Buzz seemed taken in by it all. "What a nice bear!" he said.

"And he smells like strawberries!" added Rex.

Oh, brother, I thought.

Lotso led us to a bathroom door. It opened and a gigantic baby doll came out. His name was Big Baby. He was pretty intimidating. He was taller than any other toy in the place and covered in ball-point-pen tattoos. Lotso told us that he and Big Baby had once had the same owner, before they were both abandoned.

Lotso led us through the bathroom to another classroom. "And here's where you folks will be staying—the Caterpillar Room!" he announced.

The place was full of kid stuff— small tables and chairs, finger paintings, wooden blocks, cubbies with wire-mesh bins, alphabet banners. A colorful toy train circled the room, blowing its whistle merrily.

"Look at this place!" cried Jessie, her eyes shining.

"Jackpot, baby!" crowed Mr. Potato Head.

Then Lotso said the words my friends had been dying to hear. "In a few minutes that bell's going to ring, and you'll get the playtime that you've been dreaming of."

Rex nearly lost it. "Play! Real play! I can't wait!" he squealed.

"Now, if you'll excuse me," said Lotso, "we'd best be heading back. Welcome to Sunnyside, folks!"

My friends were beside themselves with happiness. "Thank you, Mr. Lotso!" they called. "Thank you! Goodbye!"

After Lotso and his gang left, the toys turned to the windows. We could hear the sounds of kids playing.

"Oh, I want to get played with!" cried Rex. "Why can't time go faster?"

"How many do you reckon are out there?" Jessie wondered.

"Oh, they sound so sweet!" said Mrs. Potato Head.

The toys were so excited. All they wanted

to do was get played with. Sunnyside did seem great. But we belonged to Andy. We belonged *with* Andy.

"Look, everyone, it's nice here, I admit," I said. "But we need to go home now."

The toys all exchanged glances. They thought I was nuts.

Then Jessie spoke up. "We can have a new life here, Woody. A chance to make kids happy again."

"Yes! Stay here!" all the toys called out.

"I can't," I said. But they continued to talk. "Guys, really—NO!" It came out louder than I had meant it to. My friends looked taken aback.

But I couldn't help it. I was upset and fed up. "I *have* a kid . . . *you* have a kid—Andy! And our job is to be there for him! If he wants us at college, or in the attic, well then, that's where we should be! Now, I'm going home. Anyone who wants to join me is welcome." I turned to the one toy I knew would be on my side. "Come on, Buzz!"

I started to walk away. But Buzz didn't follow me.

"Buzz . . . ?" I asked, stunned.

Buzz looked me dead in the eye. "Our mission with Andy is complete, Woody," he said gently. "And what's important now is that we stay together."

I stared at him in disbelief. "We wouldn't even be together if it weren't for Andy! Look under your boot, Buzz! You too, Jessie! Whose name is written there, huh?"

Finally Rex spoke up. "Maybe Andy doesn't care about us anymore," he said sadly.

"What?" I sputtered. "Of course he cares about us! He cares about all of you! He was putting you in the attic! I saw. You can't just turn your back on him now!"

Jessie shook her head. "Woody, wake up! It's over. Andy's grown up!"

I looked around at my friends. It was suddenly perfectly clear—I was on my own. The toys were going to stay at Sunnyside and there was nothing I could do about it.

"So this is it?" I asked. "After all we've been through?"

Buzz stepped forward and held out his hand. But I was too mad to shake it. I adjusted my hat and walked to the door. I had to get home before Andy took off for college.

And I would have to go alone.

There I stood, trapped on Sunnyside's roof. It hadn't been easy getting out of the daycare center. After leaving my friends in the Caterpillar Room, I'd hitched a ride on the janitor's cart and made it as far as the bathroom. Then I shinnied out the bathroom window and climbed up to the roof.

But once I got up there, I realized that the wall surrounding the playground was too far away for me to jump over. I didn't have any idea how I'd get down.

The breeze picked up, blowing my hat off my head. As I chased after it, I spotted an old kite on the roof. *That's it!* I thought.

Holding the kite above me like a hang glider, I took a deep breath, ran across the roof, and leaped off the edge. I soared over the playground and over the high wall that surrounded it.

Yippee, I thought as I glided down for a smooth landing. *This is a piece of— Whoa!*

A gust of wind yanked me high up into the air. I rose higher and higher, until the kids on the playground looked like tiny dots.

Just then, the kite's crossbar snapped in two. I tried to flap the broken bits of kite like wings, but it was no use. I plunged toward the ground.

Luckily, a tree broke my fall. I swear, I hit each and every branch on my way down. I came to a stop just inches from the pavement.

Whew! That was a close one!

"Reach for the sky!" said a voice—*my* voice, actually. My pull string had gotten snagged on a tree branch, activating my voice box. That string had saved me!

But now I had a new problem: I was stuck on the branch. I twisted around, trying to get free, but there was no way down.

That's when Bonnie, the little girl we'd

seen at the front desk, came skipping up. Bonnie looked pretty surprised to see a cowboy doll hanging from a tree. She tugged on me, activating my voice box again. "You're my favorite deputy!"

Bonnie grinned. Before I knew what was happening, she had shoved me into her backpack.

"Oh, great!" I groaned. How was I going to get back to Andy's now?

When we got to Bonnie's house, she pulled me out of her backpack. She plunked me down at a small table with a bunch of other toys.

As soon as Bonnie left the room, I said, "Psst! Can you tell me where I am?"

"Shhh!" snapped a hedgehog in lederhosen.

"The guy's just asking a question," said a gruff-voiced unicorn.

"Well, excuse me," the hedgehog sniffed. "I am trying to stay in character."

The toys introduced themselves. The hedgehog was Mr. Pricklepants. The unicorn's name was Buttercup. There was also a plastic triceratops named Trixie, some plush peas in a pod, and a helpful doll named Dolly.

Just then, Bonnie came back and playtime started.

It had been so long since I'd been played with, I'd almost forgotten how great it could be.

Bonnie was terrific. She took us all on a wild adventure, with a witch, poisoned jelly beans, and a flying spaceship. I almost felt like I was back in the good old days with Andy— it was that much fun. I felt more alive than I had in years.

But as incredible as playtime with Bonnie had been, I knew in my heart that I belonged with Andy. I needed to find out where I was so that I could figure out how to get back to him.

That night, while Bonnie was sleeping, I slipped out from under the covers. I climbed on a chair and took a look at the address written on her backpack: 1225 Sycamore.

Bonnie's toys were watching me from the bed. "Psst! Woody! What are you doing?" Mr. Pricklepants called softly.

"I have to get out of here," I explained.

"You're leaving?" Buttercup asked in surprise. "Didn't you have fun today?"

I smiled just thinking about it. "Of course I did! More than I've had in years. But, you see,

I belong to someone else." I held up my boot so they could see Andy's name scrawled on the bottom. "And he's leaving soon. I have to get home!"

"Where's home?" asked one of the peas.

"Elm Street," I told him. Or was it her? "Two thirty-four Elm." I thought for a moment. "You guys have a map?"

Trixie the triceratops helped me pull up a map on the computer. And would you believe it? I was right around the corner from home!

I hugged Bonnie's toys and did a little victory dance.

"Oh, hey, listen," I said as I headed for the door. "If any of you guys ever get to Sunnyside Daycare, you tell them Woody made it home!"

The toys all gasped. "You came from Sunnyside?" Mr. Pricklepants asked in a terrible voice.

I froze, one boot out the door. "Yeah, there was this mix-up and—"

"But how did you escape?" asked Trixie, her eyes wide.

"Well, it wasn't easy, I . . . wait." I was getting a bad feeling. "What do you mean, 'escape'?"

I saw the toys exchange nervous glances. "Sunnyside is a place of ruin and despair, ruled by an evil bear who smells of strawberries," Mr. Pricklepants informed me.

I could hardly believe my ears. "Lotso?"

"He may seem plush and huggable on the outside," Buttercup warned, "but inside, he's a monster!"

"But how do you know that?" I asked.

"Chuckles," said Mr. Pricklepants, pointing to a broken toy clown sitting on the windowsill. "He'll tell you!"

Chuckles told me the whole sad story. Once, many years before, Chuckles, Lotso, and Big Baby had belonged to a little girl named Daisy. She had loved them all, but Lotso was her special favorite.

One day, Daisy's family went for a drive.

They stopped at a rest stop. After lunch, Daisy fell asleep, and her parents accidentally drove off without her toys. The toys waited and waited, but Daisy never came back to get them.

Lotso never gave up. He was determined to get back to Daisy. The toys walked and walked. Finally, they made it home. They were muddy, wet, and tired, but happy—until Lotso looked through the window of Daisy's room.

There was Daisy, with a brand-new Lots-o'-Huggin' Bear in her arms. Lotso had been replaced.

Something changed inside Lotso that day. Something snapped. Big Baby wanted to go inside, but Lotso wouldn't let him. "She doesn't want you anymore!" Lotso told Big Baby.

Chuckles showed me an old heart-shaped pendant that read MY HEART BELONGS TO DAISY. The pendant had belonged to Big Baby. That night, outside Daisy's house, Lotso had ripped it off the doll's neck. As Lotso saw it, Daisy had betrayed them all.

The toys were all on their own now.

After that, Lotso found his way to Sunnyside and took charge. The bitter bear made sure all the new toys got placed in the Caterpillar Room with the littlest kids so they would get destroyed. Lotso and his gang stayed in the Butterfly Room with the older kids, who knew how to play gently with toys.

New toys at Sunnyside didn't stand a chance.

When Chuckles was done with his story, I took a deep breath. I was so close to Andy! But my friends needed my help.

I knew what I had to do.

I returned to Sunnyside the way I'd left—as a stowaway in Bonnie's backpack. When the coast was clear, I slipped out of the bag and made my way to the Caterpillar Room. I hid and watched what was going on.

It was even worse than I had imagined. One kid was using Rex's head to hammer a square peg into a round hole. Another smashed the poor Potato Heads onto the floor. Another kid pretended Jessie was an airplane and launched her into the wall. *Ouch!*

Ring-ring. A cute toy telephone rolled over to me and bumped against my boot. He seemed to be trying to tell me something.

I picked up the receiver and held it to my ear. "Uh . . . hello?"

"You shouldn't have come back, cowboy. You and your friends aren't ever getting out of here now," the phone said in a tough and weary voice.

That phone had been at Sunnyside for years. He knew everything there was to know about it.

"There's only one way toys leave this place," the phone told me. He pointed out the trash chute across the yard, where the janitor was dropping off a load of trash. We watched a crushed toy train disappear into the chute.

"Trash truck comes at dawn," said the phone. "Then it's off to the dump."

I shuddered. That poor, poor train.

But I couldn't let that stop me. I told the phone my friends and I were leaving, no matter what. "If you'd help us, I'd sure be grateful."

With a sigh, the toy told me what we'd have to do to get out of Sunnyside. There were doors to unlock, walls to climb, patrol trucks to avoid—and that wasn't all.

"Your real problem is the Monkey," said

the phone. The Monkey sat at the front desk, watching the security monitors all night long. "You can unlock doors, sneak past guards, climb the wall," the phone told me. "But if you don't take out that monkey, you're not going anywhere. You want to get out of here? Get rid of that monkey!"

Finally, it was recess time. The kids dropped the toys and ran outside. My friends sat up, groaning in pain.

"Psst! Psst! Hey, guys!" I called from behind a puppet theater.

Were they glad to see me! "Thank goodness!" cried Mrs. Potato Head.

"You're alive!" exclaimed Slinky Dog.

"Of course I'm alive." I looked around. Someone was missing. "Wait, where's Buzz?"

"Lotso did something to him!" said Rex.

"He thinks he's the real Buzz Lightyear!" explained Slinky. Turns out Buzz had been reprogrammed. He thought his friends were galactic enemies. And now he was helping Lotso!

My heart sank. Buzz, my good friend, had been turned against us!

"Oh, Woody," said Jessie, hanging her head. "We were wrong to leave Andy. I was wrong."

I shook my head. "No, it's my fault for leaving you guys. From now on, we stick together." That was what Buzz had wanted all along. And now I knew he'd been right.

"But Andy's leaving for college," said Slinky, my faithful friend.

Jessie gasped. "College! We've got to get you home before Andy leaves tomorrow!"

"Tomorrow?" said Hamm. "But that means . . ."

I locked eyes with Jessie and nodded. "It means we're busting out of here tonight."

We spent the rest of the afternoon preparing. That night, after the doors were locked and the kids had gone home, we put our plan into action.

My friends had been right about Buzz— Lotso had turned him into a mindless robot. Every evening, Buzz locked the rest of Andy's toys into wire-mesh bins. Then he stood guard over them all night long.

But that night, during roll call, Mr. Potato Head pretended to try to escape out the window. Buzz nabbed him.

Of course, this was all part of our plan to distract the Monkey. While the Monkey was watching Mr. Potato Head on the video monitors, Slinky sneaked up through a panel in the ceiling. I was waiting there for him. Then Slink and I made our way to the office. We tackled the Monkey and tied him up with Scotch tape so he couldn't sound the alert.

After we found the key to the Caterpillar Room, Slinky climbed on top of the desk and moved one of the security cameras from side to side. That was the signal to Jessie to start the next part of our plan: Faking a Fight.

Hamm and Rex began arguing and pushing each other. When Buzz came in to break up the fight, Jessie and Bullseye dropped a toy bin over him.

Meanwhile, Barbie moved on to Phase Three: Getting Info from Ken. With sobs and tears, she told Ken she couldn't take life in prison anymore. He fell for it and invited her to his dollhouse. But that Barbie is tougher than she looks. She tied Ken up and made him tell her how to switch Buzz back to normal.

While Barbie was taking care of Ken, Slinky and I were sneaking past the toy trucks that

patrolled Sunnyside. Slinky used a rubber band to slingshot the room key under the door.

Jessie caught the key and unlocked the door. Then Jessie, Mrs. Potato Head, Bullseye, and the Aliens quietly slipped outside.

Up to that point, everything had gone perfectly. But then Buzz escaped.

"Stop him!" I yelled. "Don't let him get out!"

As he ran, Buzz pressed a button on his chest. "Star Command, I am approaching the escape hatch," he announced. "Prepare for liftoff!" Poor Buzz—he didn't even recognize his friends anymore. He thought he was in outer space. We had to fix him right away!

Hamm and Rex let out a war cry and tackled Buzz. Fortunately, Barbie arrived with Buzz's control manual.

"Quick, open his back!" I cried. "There's a switch!"

"Unhand me, Zurg scum," commanded Buzz. "The galactic courts will show you no mercy!"

I flipped the switch back and forth. "It's not working! Why is it not working?"

We tried to reset Buzz. But something went wrong. He whipped around and pointed his laser at my forehead.

"*¿Amigo o enemigo?*" he asked. *Uh-oh.*

We'd switched him into Spanish mode!

I opened my arms to show him I meant no harm. "Uh . . . *amigos*," I said. "We're all amigos!"

That satisfied him. He walked up to me and kissed me on each cheek.

Ay, caramba!

I had no idea how we were going to change Buzz back. But I decided we'd figure that out later. Right now we had to move on to the last phase of our plan: Making Our Way to the Trash Chute—and Freedom.

We all sneaked onto the playground, creeping past Lotso's patrol. It wasn't easy, but we finally made it to the chute.

With some help from El Buzzo, we opened the chute door and boosted each other up. I climbed inside and peered down. It was dark and scary.

"Is it safe?" asked Jessie.

"I guess I'll find out." I let go of the chute's rim and slid down. I came to a stop at the bottom of the chute, teetering on the edge of a big trash bin. Below my feet was a pit of darkness.

"Woody? You okay?" called Jessie.

"Come on down," I called back. "But not all at once."

The next thing I knew, I could hear them sliding down—all at once!

"No, no, no, no, no, no!" I yelled. They

nearly knocked me into the Dumpster. I spun my arms as I tried to keep from falling. Luckily, Jessie grabbed me and pulled me to safety.

"Thanks, Jess," I said gratefully.

I turned to Slinky and pointed to the other side of the Dumpster. All we had to do was cross it, and then we'd be free. "Slink? Think you can make it?"

"I might be old," said Slinky Dog. "But I've still got a spring in my step." He backed up, took a few steps, and leaped over the open pit. He grabbed a metal handle on the other side. His spring body formed a bridge across the Dumpster.

I grinned. Attaboy!

"Okay," Slinky called. "Climb across!"

But before we could even take a step, Slinky gasped. Two furry pink legs stepped out of the darkness in front of him. Lotso had found us!

Uh-oh. Lotso kicked Slinky's paws out from under him. Luckily, we were able to pull Slinky to safety.

Lotso's gang stepped up behind him. We tried to escape back up the garbage chute. But Stretch, Lotso's octopus thug, blocked our way. We were trapped.

"What are you all doing?" Lotso asked, shaking his head in disbelief. "Running back to your kid? He doesn't care about you!"

"That's a lie!" I shouted.

"Is it?" taunted Lotso. "Tell me this, cowboy: if your kid loves you so much, why is he going away?"

Lotso turned to the rest of the toys. "It's the same for every toy!" he exclaimed. "Used and abandoned! You think you're special? You're a piece of plastic. You were made to be thrown away!"

Vroom! As if on cue, a garbage truck turned into the alley and began rumbling toward us. Everyone gasped.

"Speak of the devil," said Lotso with an evil smile. "Now, we need toys in our Caterpillar Room, and you need to avoid that truck. Why don't you come back and join our family again?"

Jessie stepped forward. "This isn't a family, it's a prison!" she cried. "You're a liar and a bully and I'd rather rot in this Dumpster than join any family of yours!"

Lotso smirked. "Well, if that's what you want." He gave the signal. Stretch began to push us toward the edge of the Dumpster!

"Wait!" I cried. "What about Daisy?"

Lotso tried to play it off. "I don't know what you're talking about," he said coolly.

"Daisy—you used to do everything with her," I said.

"And then she threw me out!" he shouted.

"No, she lost you. By accident." I reached into my holster and pulled out the old pendant Chuckles had given me. The one that had belonged to Big Baby. Even though the

pendant was faded, you could still make out the words: MY HEART BELONGS TO DAISY.

Lotso's mouth fell open. "Where did you get that?" he asked.

I saw my chance. "She loved you, Lotso. As much as any kid ever loved a toy!" I threw the pendant at him. It landed at his feet.

Lotso's face crumpled. "She never loved me. She left me!" he roared. "Love means being together forever. Or it isn't love!"

Big Baby picked up the pendant. His lower lip trembled. "Mama!" he cried. A tear ran down his cheek.

This made Lotso furious. "What, you want your mama back?" he taunted. "She never loved you. Don't be such a baby!" He snatched the pendant from Big Baby and crushed it with the end of his cane.

"Push them all in!" Lotso yelled to his gang. "We're all just trash, waiting to be thrown away. That's all a toy is!"

I thought it was the end for us. But then,

to my amazement, Big Baby grabbed Lotso. He lifted him over his head.

"Ahhh!" Lotso screamed. "Put me down!"

Big Baby tossed the rotten bear into the Dumpster and slammed the lid. For a moment, there was stunned silence. Then everyone— even the members of Lotso's gang—cheered.

That was our cue to exit. The garbage truck was getting closer. We hopped onto the lid of the Dumpster and ran to the other side.

I was almost across when I heard a squeak. I turned. One of the Aliens was stuck in the crack between the two halves of the lid.

I ran back and yanked him free. But as I tried to run, something stopped me. A familiar pink paw had a death grip on my leg. Lotso! He pulled me down into the dark Dumpster.

The garbage truck's brakes squealed. I heard a loud rumble as it picked up the Dumpster.

The Dumpster began to tilt. I knew I was about to be thrown into the garbage truck. I grabbed on to the lid. When it swung open,

I saw Jessie. I reached my hand out and she grabbed it! But the flow of trash was too strong. Jessie lost her grip, and I fell into the garbage truck. And then Jessie and the rest of my friends fell in, too!

We landed in a heap of trash. It was dark, disgusting, and stinky. "Can you hear me?" I called. "Is everyone okay?"

"Of course not, you imbecile!" called Mr. Potato Head. "We're doomed!"

In the darkness, I spotted Buzz in the middle of a heap of trash. (He glows in the dark, you know.) "Everyone! Go to Buzz! C'mon!" I shouted.

I took a quick head count. We were all there. Just then, the truck stopped for another pickup. I realized that more garbage was on its way!

"Against the wall, everybody!" I yelled. "Quick!"

We all pressed ourselves against the wall. But where was Jessie? Buzz heard her voice and raced over to save her. He picked her up and started running toward us.

The trash began to pour in. We looked up. *Oh, no!* An old TV set crashed down from above. It was heading right for them!

Buzz threw Jessie to the side just before the TV hit. *SMASH!*

It took all of us to lift the heavy TV. Slinky found Buzz and pulled him out. He wasn't moving.

"Buzz!" Jessie cried, shaking him. "Buzz!"

Suddenly, with a loud beep, Buzz came back to life.

"Oh, Buzz!" shouted Jessie. She threw her arms around him. "You're back! You're back, you're back, you're back!"

"Yes, I'm back!" said Buzz. He looked confused. "Where have I been?"

"Beyond infinity, space ranger." I put my hand on Buzz's shoulder. It was good to see my friend back to his old self.

Buzz smiled. But then he took a look around. "So . . . where are we now?"

"In a garbage truck on the way to the dump!" exclaimed Rex.

The smile on Buzz's face vanished.

The truck lurched to a halt at the Tri-County Landfill. There was a grinding noise, and suddenly we found ourselves sliding out.

"Hold on!" I shouted. "We're going in!"

We landed at the base of a trash heap. The landfill was the most awful place I'd ever seen. Mountains of trash stretched in every direction. A foul-smelling breeze blew through the air.

The Aliens popped up from the trash heap. One of them pointed to a big crane in the distance. "The Claw!" they exclaimed in unison.

I squinted. It did look a lot like the claw from the arcade game in Pizza Planet, where Buzz and I had first met the Aliens. The Aliens started to run toward it.

"Hey, guys, no!" I yelled. We needed to stick together! But it was too late. A huge bulldozer rumbled over, pushing us out of the way.

"Hang on!" I cried as we were swept up in a wave of garbage. We tumbled around in the tide of trash.

Just when I thought I couldn't take any more, we landed on a conveyor belt. We were heading into a dark tunnel. I had a feeling the worst was yet to come.

"Woody, what do we do?" Mrs. Potato Head asked, panicked.

"Everything will be okay as long as we stay toge—" I started to say.

Whoosh! Slinky Dog was pulled straight up into the air. He stuck to a fast-moving conveyor belt, high above us.

All around me, cans and other metal objects started flying up and sticking to the conveyor belt. "It's a magnet!" I realized. "Watch out!"

"Whoa! Woody!" Slinky exclaimed. From high up, he could see what was coming. The belt we were on was heading right toward a garbage shredder!

We realized we needed to be on the same belt as Slinky! "Quick!" called Buzz. "Grab something metal!"

He grabbed a lunch box and was pulled up.

I grabbed a doorknob and flew up next. Everyone else made it, too. We were safe—at least for the moment.

Then I heard someone cry, "Help! Help me!"

I looked down and saw Lotso pinned under a golf bag.

"I'm stuck! Help! Please! Help!" he cried.

Yes, Lotso was the reason we were here. He was mean, plain and simple. But I couldn't just leave him there to face the shredder. No one deserved that.

I let go of the doorknob and fell back onto the belt. I ran to Lotso and tried to lift the golf bag, but it was too heavy. Buzz dropped down to help me. Together, we managed to free Lotso. We grabbed hold of a golf club and were sucked up to safety just in time.

"Thank you, Sheriff," said Lotso.

I nodded. "We're all in this together."

We passed over the shredder and landed on another conveyor belt. In the distance we could see a bright glow.

"I can see daylight!" said Rex. "We're gonna be okay!"

Everyone scrambled forward, excited. But as we got closer, I froze. The glow we saw at the end was not the rising sun. It was the red-hot molten center of the dump's incinerator!

"Run!" I screamed.

We ran for our lives. But there was nowhere to go. Smooth walls surrounded the conveyor belt on all sides.

Lotso managed to grab a ladder built into the wall. An emergency stop button was high above him. It was our only chance.

Buzz, Jessie, and I boosted Lotso onto the ladder. "Hurry!" I cried.

Lotso began to climb. At last he reached the glowing blue button. He stopped and looked down at us. We couldn't outrun the conveyor belt much longer. "Just push it!" I shouted.

Lotso didn't move.

"PUSH IT!" thundered Buzz.

Lotso dropped his arm.

I couldn't believe it. He was going to leave us! "No! No! NO!" I cried.

Lotso saluted me, a smirk on his furry face. Where's your 'Andy' now?" he sneered.

Then he ran away.

"Lotso!" Buzz screamed as he slid off the end of the conveyor belt.

And then I was falling, too. "Noooo!" I yelled.

We landed on a slope of trash that was sliding

toward the fiery pit. The heat was unbearable. No matter how fast we climbed, we couldn't escape the tide of garbage.

There was nothing left to do. So we all joined hands. We would face this together.

As I closed my eyes, I had one last thought: *If this is the end, at least I'm with my friends.*

Over the deafening roar of the incinerator, I heard another sound. My eyes snapped open. I was shocked to see a giant metal claw lowering toward us. It scooped us up just before we reached the roaring flames.

But . . . how? When I looked over, I saw the Aliens in the booth of the crane. They were manning the controls of "the Claw"!

The next thing I knew, the claw dropped us onto the ground. We were all groaning and coughing. But we were safe.

And Lotso? We never found out what happened to him. I suppose it doesn't really matter.

Mr. Potato Head lay on his back, staring at the sky. "You know all that bad stuff I said about

Andy's attic? I take it all back," he said.

We all agreed.

"Come on, Woody!" said Jessie. "We gotta get you home."

"That's right, college boy!" said Buzz.

"But what about you guys?" I said. "I mean, maybe the attic's not such a great idea." I didn't want to tell my friends what to do. They needed to do what was best for them.

"We're Andy's toys," said Jessie.

"We'll be there for him," Buzz agreed. "Together."

I felt relieved. But how would we get to Andy's? That's when we spotted our friendly neighborhood garbageman. We sneaked into the truck and were home before we knew it.

We arrived just in time. Andy was loading up the car to leave for college! We rinsed off the dirt from the dump with the garden hose and quickly made our way upstairs. There wasn't a minute to lose!

My friends climbed into a box labeled ATTIC.

I headed for the COLLEGE box. But just before I scrambled inside, I stopped and walked to my friends. This could be the last time I saw them. Ever.

"Buzz," I said.

Buzz turned around. We shook hands.

"This isn't goodbye," I said. There was so much more I wanted to say. But I didn't even know where to start.

Buzz understood. "You know where to find us, cowboy," he told me with a smile.

I heard footsteps. Andy was coming! I gave my old pal Buzz a salute. Then we both ducked into our boxes. But as I climbed in, my heart was heavy. Something was not quite right.

Andy and his mom came into the room. Andy's mom was having a hard time saying goodbye, too. "Oh, Andy," she said. "I wish I could always be with you."

"You will be, Mom," Andy said, hugging her.

Andy's words echoed in my head. Suddenly, everything was clear to me. I knew what I had to do.

When Andy went out to the hallway, I jumped out of the box and grabbed a marker and a sticky note. I crossed out ATTIC and wrote another address on the box. I finished just before Andy got back.

Andy got out of his car, carrying the box of toys. He stopped in front of a small house with a neat lawn and a white picket fence. Andy checked the address against the one I had written on the box: 1225 Sycamore.

A little girl was playing in the front yard. "No! Don't go in there!" she said in a scary voice. "The bakery is haunted!" It was Bonnie playing another one of her wonderfully wacky games.

Andy said hello to Bonnie's mother. Then he leaned down to talk to Bonnie.

"I'm Andy," he said to her. "Someone told me you're really good with toys. These are mine, but I'm going away now, so I need someone really special to look after them."

He opened the box and began to pull the toys out. Jessie and Bullseye. Rex. The Potato Heads. Slinky. Hamm. The Aliens. Buzz. Andy introduced them to Bonnie one by one.

"Now, you gotta promise to take good care of these guys," he said when he'd handed

over all the toys—except for me.

Bonnie looked into the box and said, "My cowboy!"

Andy looked down. "Woody? What's he doing in here?"

That's right, I had decided to come along, too! You see, I'd realized that no matter where I went, I would always be with Andy. I didn't need to be sitting on his dorm room shelf to be near him.

Bonnie eagerly reached for me. But Andy pulled me back. He sighed and looked down at me. Then he nodded and held me out for Bonnie to see.

"Now, Woody's been my pal for as long as I can remember," he told Bonnie. "He's brave, like a cowboy should be, and kind and smart. But the thing that makes Woody special is that he'll never give up on you—ever. He'll be there for you, no matter what. You think you can take care of him for me?"

Bonnie nodded seriously.

"Okay, then." He handed me over. Bonnie hugged me close.

And then it happened. After all those years of patiently waiting in the toy box, the moment we all had been wishing for came. Andy played with us again! He grabbed Hamm first. "Oh, no!" he said. "Dr. Porkchop is attacking the haunted bakery!"

Bonnie joined right in. "Oh, no! The ghosts are getting away!" She put on her Woody voice. "Woody to the rescue!"

It was just as amazing as we had imagined it would be. Playing with our old pal, knowing it was the last playtime we'd have with him.

Afterward, we all agreed: it had been the perfect way to say goodbye to Andy.

Before long, Andy had to go. He walked toward his car, then turned for one last look at us. He smiled softly and said goodbye.

I had a lump in my throat. "So long, pardner," I whispered. Buzz put his arm around my shoulders. The other toys gathered around us. We watched Andy's car until it disappeared.

I took a deep breath. I would always miss Andy. But he was moving on. And it was time for us to move on, too. Now we belonged to a little girl named Bonnie. And our new adventures were about to begin.